Synz Two: Remixed & Reloaded

By Inakat

© Inakat 2013

Detroit, MI

Adult Reading Material

The Synz Series

I *Synz En Detroit*

II *Synz : Remixed and Reloaded January 2013*

Other Works by Inakat

How Day Getz it Done *June 2009*

Sasha N. Deeplee *March 2011*

Smoking Hot Panties (Book 1) *October 2012*

High Maintenance Assests *November 2012*

Website: http://www.inakat1.com

Facebook: www.facebook.com/InakatPublishing

Twittet http://www.twitter.com/Inakat1 **or** @Inakat1

"Mother, that's none of your business. Besides you may finally learn something about me." Dan said.

"I learned something about you when Paula left. How is she by the way?" Lori asked.

"I haven't heard from her." "It seems that no one has heard from her since she left."

Lori folded her arms and frowned at Dan. Whatever emotion that his mother had hoped for from Dan was wasted. He didn't blink, grimace or even smile. By the look on his face he was indifferent to Paula's absence. Lori craned her neck towards Synz.

Inakat Publishing

Copywrite © Inakat Publishing 2012

First Printing Jan 2013

This book is dedicated to the only people that I've ever truly loved. You know who you are, there was a never a reason to ask. Now you know how much.

Chapter One

Synz rolled on the bed and groaned. Her hand went down to her bloated midsection and rubbed gently. She swung her feet out of the bed and reached over to switch the lamp on. Synz's wiggled her feet into her furry black house shoes. Soft light filled the room as she rubbed her eyes and stretched.

She gripped her thighs tightly and leaned back on her knuckles to steady herself as she pushed off the mattress. Nubby carpet cushioned her feet as she stepped quickly into the bathroom. Synz's flipped the toilet seat down and steadied herself carefully on to it.

When she was done, she made her way to the sink to wash her hands and examine her. She turned on the vanity light above the sink and giggled at her reflection. Her sheer pink and blue nightgown had risen to her thighs and fit snugly. Her nose shined with oil and her cheeks had become pudgy.

Synz sighed as she made her way from the bathroom. She grabbed her housecoat before she made her way to the kitchen. It had been a few hours since had left the house in rush. He hadn't to bother to explain where he was going to Synz.

Sinclair Welch was twenty-eight years old and married to a man ten years her senior. She'd finally learned some things about her new husbands prior life. He'd been raised in a two parent home, was born in Manhattan, New York but his family had moved to Bloomfield, Michigan when he was two years old. His father was absent most of the time and his mother either didn't notice or simply didn't care.

His mother Lori Ann was homemaker, and his father Ezra had inherited several thousand acres of rented farmland that had spanned across the states of Alabama, Georgia, and Mississippi. Ezra had spent a good deal of his time gone to oversee those properties and to acquire new pieces of land.

Since Ezra had made the bulk of his monies from the rentals of the land, he'd gone above and beyond to ensure that his tenants met the qualifications to be enrolled in programs that were government subsidized.

Ezra's appeared to be a talented businessman on the surface, when in fact he'd kept the plan very simple. If a farm property could grow enough of a particular high quality fruit, vegetable or livestock that would pass or exceed the United States Department of Agricultures rules and regulations, then that farmer was could participate in their programs.

Program participation ensured that the farm had buyer for its product and would be paid regularly upon harvest. Those funds would then be used to pay for land rentals, equipment, employees, and provide other essentials for the day to day upkeep of the farms.

Whatever Ezra did in his travels had provided Lori Ann plenty to raise and care for the household in his absence. He'd purchased the five bedroom home in Bloomfield to move her and Daniel to a place that he'd believe was more progressive than Southern states. However, he practically dumped his family in the North and spent the majority of his life in South, away from them.

Chapter Two

Once Dan got his hands on a portion of the family finances, he'd quickly invested it in the rise of on screen pornography and technology. Shortly after he'd seen his first major flow of profits from those businesses, he then began to divest his earnings into other forms of entertainment. By the time he'd stumbled across Synz Dan was a thirty five year old man that had only been married very briefly once and had no children.

He'd had his pick of beautiful, educated women to chose from before he'd seen her. Something about inner fire had caused him to seek her above all. The fact that she'd shown him that spit-fire attitude of hers was an added plus. He'd grown used to women that went out of their way to cater to please him and Synz just wouldn't, even after she'd known about his fortune.

Dan hadn't had many people he was close to as the ages rolled by him. He'd always lacked the ability to connect to other humans in an emotional way. To him people were objects like toys or shoes. They were replaceable. Whenever Dan showed a hint of emotion it was usually anger or disapproval. Over the years he'd learned to mimic what others did in situations that called to show what he was supposed to have felt. Nevertheless, the sentiments he expressed weren't genuine rather than short acts for onlookers.

By the time he only five years old, it was apparent that something was amiss inside of him. After his mother had been called to the school about images he'd drawn, she began to take him to church. Even in her refusal to admit to school authorities that there may be a problem, she'd chosen to handle it in the only way she'd known how. Lori believed that he lacked a belief in a higher power and thought that some form of religion would cure whatever ailed her child.

Still Lori was permissive when came to Dan. Whenever he'd tested the lines of authority, Lori declined to discipline him. Instead, she'd helped cover up his ill behavior. Lori didn't want the disturbed actions of her child to see the light of day. For her it was a reflection on her skills as a parent. She'd been taught to never speak ill of family and to always uphold the family image regardless of the situation. In turn that decision had given her first born child and only son a chance to thrive in darkness unchecked.

Dan had never had friends or been considered a friendly child. His bossy and arrogant nature had left him isolated from his peers from the start. When Lori at his Ezra insistence signed him up to play baseball on a community league in order to socialize him was called out by the coach about his temper, she removed him from the team before he'd ever played a game. She'd hidden the fact that no longer played ball from his father, and allowed him to spend time alone in the massive woods behind their home, whenever Ezra happened to be at home to cover further cover her lie.

Dan's mean-spirited nature had began to show so severely, that by the seventh grade, she hired a tutor and started a home school program. By then he'd already been excluded several times for the same reasons, violence against other children. Usually because he'd envied something that they had and had decided to take it. When the other refused to hand over whatever Dan had wanted, he would attack them viciously and without provocation.

After he'd been removed from school, Lori was sure that he would settle down and find himself. When Ezra questioned why the boy had pulled from school, again Lori covered up for her son. She'd told his father that Dan was too smart for the material that the school offered and since they could afford to pay for a private tutor there was no need to hold Dan back.

Had Ezra been around more often he would have known what his son's issues were. Lori had know that if he'd found out exactly what had gone on, his father wouldn't have hesitated to lock Dan away in the best mental institution his money could buy, in place of the funds used for a private tutor.

Chapter Three

Subsequent to his removal from mainstream society around him, at thirteen Dan began to face puberty alone. He'd no friends to snicker and fantasize with, no adults that took a real interest in him and to make matters worse his mother had just given birth to a set of twin girls. The only person that he'd had consistently in his life was busy with two small children.

He didn't hate the twins, but was indifferent to their birth. There was a slight envy that his mother would now put him on hold to care and fuss about them. He took no interest in a role of brotherhood in anyway. By the time he'd turned fifteen. the two busy toddlers were a bit much for him to swallow. They'd developed a habit that annoyed him to no end.

They wanted to love up their big brother. Again, Dan didn't understand the desire for attention or affection from the matched little people. He'd right away began to pinch and hit them whenever they came near. His mother had finally become aware that Dan's problems had nothing to do with the world around him. She'd known the girls were harmless little bundles of joy.

Once Dan had proved to her that he was capable of hurting his own flesh and blood, Lori had become afraid of him. No longer was he a pudgy little, selfish kid, but had grown to be nearly six feet tall and yet he weighed close to two hundred pounds. She'd kept the girls away from any alone time with him.

It was on Dan's seventeenth birthday that Lori had given up on him. Dinner time had come and she'd had fresh Maine Lobster flown in for the occasion. It had always been his favorite food and she'd planned to have a quiet cookout in the backyard with the just her and the children. The girls were in their bedroom with their dollies and played together quietly as they waited for their mother's call.

Lori had called for Dan several times from the backdoor. When he didn't respond, she reluctantly decided that he must have been too far in the woods to hear her. She would have to go get him. She crossed the lush green grass and ventured into the line of trees that signaled the end of a clear path.

Chapter Four

She'd only gone about a hundred yards into the forest-like area before she'd spotted Dan. He sat on the ground cover in blood. Lori raced to him to see if he was hurt. The metallic stench of fresh blood stung her nostrils just as a clear view of Dan into her view.

 Dan didn't acknowledge his mother's presence. Lori was only four feet from him when she stopped in her tracks and recoiled in horror. Dan sat serenely in pile of bloody intestines. A few feet away lay the remnants of a slaughtered deer. A Scant inches from Dan's feet laid the beheaded remains of fully developed fawn. Lori's gut wrenching screams snapped Dan out his trance-like state.

When he'd come to, he slowly got up and asked her was it time to eat dinner. Lori backed away from him and ran into the house. The party was cancelled as she sat locked in her room with the twins for the remainder of the day. Lori found she couldn't close her eyes to sleep all night long.

Come daybreak she'd called the tutor and offered her fifteen thousand to sign off on Dan's education. By noon Lori had arranged lodging and entrance into California State University in Northridge, CA. She put him on the Greyhound Bus line by three in the afternoon, headed three thousand miles away from her and the girls.

Lori cut off all communication with Dan other than to send him money to sustain himself. That fall, Ezra died of massive coronary. It was then that Lori discovered two things. First, that her absent husband had willed sixty percent of his estate to his only son Daniel, and two that he'd also willed ten percent of his estate to his Mistress and child four daughters in Biloxi, Mississippi. The rest would provide a comfortable life for her and the girls.

Upon Ezra's death, the property that she lived in had been paid off by an addendum of his insurance and he'd left Lori and the girls as beneficiaries of insurance policies that totaled more than forty million dollars. The only glitch for Dan was the stipulation that he must produce a minimum of a four year degree of his choice, in order to receive his inheritance. Dan graduated from college shortly before his twenty first birthday with a Bachelors' Economic Science.

Dan immediately began to take on the role of wealthy business man and quickly showed his talent to dominate others as adult. Once he'd realized that the country people that had done business with his father hated his arrogant demeanor, he understood that in order to continue to build his wealth he'd have to go in a different direction. On the day that he'd been introduced to the Board of Directors as Ezra's successor, more than two-third of them had walked out of the meeting before he was done with the new lay-out.

It hadn't seemed as if two months had passed to Synz. She thought the worst of their meeting was behind them. Dan was rich, successful, and had proven to be quite obedient behind closed doors. Synz had decided it could be easier for her to deal with him for a while; however, she would never trust him or let her guard down.

Dan had begun to show nervousness after the first week of coming home to Synz. He'd recognized that he'd miscalculated her. Deep in his gut he was waiting for the other shoe to drop. She hadn't bolted from his presence or tried to get away from him, since he'd kidnapped her. That fact that she hadn't left, even though she could, kept him worried.

He'd objected fiercely, when he learned that she'd allowed Yandi and the others to leave. Synz sat him down and explained that it was them or her. In the back of her mind she'd expected Dan to protest more, when he didn't she'd become even more suspicious of him.

Synz's past experience from the lifestyle had told her that people tended to like what they liked. Dan had shown a penchant for possessions. She understood that there was small part of him that would remain incensed that she'd made the decision to let them leave. She had hinted that they would re-build the harem, together. He'd relented and agreed.

Although Dan had spent years training the women he had, he also looked forward to the changes that Synz might bring about. The business man in him recognized that a merger was only possible if he could give some. He had hidden the main reason that he wanted her so badly. Dan had known that Synz had an ability that he didn't, a dangerous talent which came naturally to her. She'd shown a knack to draw one into her world without effort and always left you to desire her even more.

Chapter Five

She'd managed to learn quite a bit about Dan after his mother had come to visit. Lori was a small, stout woman that wore thick glasses. Her auburn and grey hair was cut in a crisp bob. The wrinkles around her eyes made it appear as if her eyes were closed, when she was awake. Synz was surprised that to find the woman quite pleasant.

It hadn't taken long for his mother to talk, without Dan him the room. Although Lori talked, Synz noticed that Lori spoke in a way that suggested she was on the defensive at all times. Synz had watched her closely when she'd come in to see her son.

She thought it was odd that Dan had opened the door for his mother, and then stood back for her to come inside the home. He smiled yet glared at his mother. Lori introduced herself to Synz and walked inside headed for the kitchen. His mother hadn't acknowledged him directly in any way. Synz was puzzled as to why they hadn't embraced or exchanged any terms of endearments.

Her concern grew when his mother informed them that she would stay at the Marriot close by. Dan didn't object or offer her the guest room. Synz told Lori that the guest room was available to her. Lori refused quickly and with a sharp tone.

"Well, you seem like a nice enough person Sinclair. How did my son manage to snag you?" Lori asked.

"Mother, that's none of your business. Besides you may finally learn something about me." Dan said.

"I learned something about you when Paula left. How is she by the way?"

"I haven't heard from her."

"It seems that no one has heard from her since she left. her own family included."

Lori folded her arms and scowled at Dan. Whatever emotion that his mother had hoped for from Dan was wasted. He didn't blink, grimace or even smile. Judging by the look on his face he was indifferent to Paula's absence. Lori craned her neck towards Synz.

Synz could only shrug her shoulders. She had never heard of Paula before then. Synz immediately guessed that Paula was Dan's love interest gone wrong. It seemed as if his mother had formed a bond with the woman and was upset with him about something related to Paula. Synz could only wait until someone said more about the woman

Chapter Six

His mother had arrived at four in the afternoon and by seven she'd left. Synz had sat with her for an hour, while Dan had taken a call from overseas in the library. Synz had hoped to learn more about Dan from his mother. However, she learned that Lori left her with more questions than answers.

"Mrs. Lori your son is quite a special piece of work. You must be proud of his success." Synz said.

"I'm satisfied that he chose a path other than prison." Lori replied.

"He seems to have a knack for business. He's a very astute in acquiring new business."

"He's very astute. He's a lot of things but he's my son. Mother warned me about his father. I was young and fool-hardy. I'd already given myself to him and become pregnant with his child. Ezra married me before I learned his family secret.

Ezra was a product of sibling lust. Dan's grandmother was also his great aunt. It was too late to do anything. I never allowed him to see those people. When Daniel was born and he looked healthy. I was sure everything would be alright. It's not my fault.

I did everything I could to help him. I did my best. Those people were a toxic mix of poor stock. I've done nothing wrong. He's my child. I'd hoped those mutant genes hadn't tainted my baby. What does any of that matter now though? He's an adult. I couldn't stop it if I wanted to. It was simply too late."

"Too late for what?"

"I'd already birthed him."

"Are you saying you never wanted Dan?"

"I said exactly what I meant. I'd already given birth. He was alive and seemed healthy. There was nothing else that I could do."

Lori face became sullen. Synz waited for Lori to finish but she didn't. When Dan returned to kitchen, he told his mother it was time for her to go. Lori got up and followed her son out the door without a word. What Synz had heard from mother had left her in amazement.

It was mornings like this one that had made Synz curious about Dan's mother statements. He was gone. When he did return, Dan would be evasive about his activities and whereabouts. Synz shook of her questions from her head and opted to get her day started. Time would reveal it all.

Synz sat down on Dan's side of the bed to retrieve a necklace. She'd removed it from Dan's neck the night before. She had come to the point where she looked forward to the impromptu sessions with him. Last night had been one of those nights. The thin gold necklace had lodged itself firmly into the carpet. The only way to retrieve it without damage was to move the nightstand and to see what was held it.

Synz pushed at the ledge of the heavy piece of furniture. It didn't budge. Her cheeks filled with air as she accepted that the thick carpet and weight of the stand had long forged and grooved together. The only way to move it was to stand up and push hard.

Synz rose up and wedge her body in between the bed and the nightstand. She shoved with all her might and the stand flipped over on its side. Her mouth flew open in surprise as the lamp went across the floor, along with other items that had rested on the top of the stand. She felt a warm trickle run down the front of her leg near her foot.

Without the lamp, Synz couldn't see very well. She went over and stood it up on the floor and reached under the shade to see if it still worked. On the first turn of the knob, the lamp came on. Synz let it sit on the floor, while she tended to what turned out to be a scratch on from the sharp end of the stand.

When she bent down to wipe the blood from her leg, she stopped. Synz rubbed her index finger in her left eye. She shook her head in disbelief as she reached under the bottom of the nightstand. Her hand trembled as she pried the tape that held a recorder and a small diary underneath the furniture.

Chapter Seven

The small cassette device was the size of a cigarette box. The device was held into place with duct tape. Synz took the book and recorder and laid them on the floor. It took two tries to lift the stand back upright, but she managed it. Synz sat on the floor and pushed the play button.

"Oh Dan, don't stop. Just that like baby, just like mommy taught you. Suck this on pacifier baby." A woman said.

"Like this mommy?" Dan asked.

"I said suck it, not talk."

"Yes ma'am."

Synz's eyes bucked as she listened. The woman sounded to be much older and her voice had a raspy, throaty, pitch to it. Dan was either very young or pretended to be a very young boy at the time that it was recorded. Synz wished very much that she knew when the tape had been made.

The tape played on in the same fashion for about fifteen minutes. There were multiple records of the different episodes of him with the same woman. Synz was perplexed when she heard the tape. She couldn't understand the significance of why he'd thought to hide it.

Synz put the recorder down and picked up the diary. From the first page, Synz was mesmerized. She'd never seen how Dan wrote other than a signature. Nevertheless, the penmanship was unmistakably masculine, and the words belonged to Dan.

Her lips moved as she read softly to herself. Her head began to swirl as the words began to form pictures in her brain. Synz balled her hand up and placed it over her mouth. Tears began to form in her eyes.

March 15th- Those bastards think they are smart. I will never be caught let alone bested by a girl. How dumb of them to send a female detective to question me. Me! I made those bitches and I alone will destroy them. I watched them on television today. They begged for her safe return. She's mine now. I shall continue to cut her up into tiny pieces and taste her flesh until, there is none left. I must keep these other whores alive so that I can continue to have alibis on hand. Today, I enjoyed a special treat. I went to her and unwrapped her. I wanted to kiss her again. The stench of her decayed flesh almost deterred me. I rinsed the bugs from her face with bottled water. A bit of her skin shed when I tried to wipe her face, but she was as beautiful as always. I want to fuck her again. I miss that. I'd kept her alive as long as I could. It's her fault. It was all her fault, if she would have shut the fuck up screaming. Why did she scream? The police were coming and I had to shut her up. I nursed at her tits. A soft jelly oozed from her. I won't be able to do it again though. Her skin has lost its elasticity. I panicked and felt the urge to bury her. She deserved a proper burial. If I allow the ground to claim her, to share her, I doubt that it will give me back the woman I gave to it. Time has become my most hated enemy. It steals from me the perfection of my creation. I've done none of the things that some of those other nitwits do. I've keep her in her entirety. Her clothes will never be found. Her body is mine, until it becomes a skeleton. Then and only then will I resurrect her. It is entirely in my control as to when and how. At last, she is completely mine.

Chapter Eight

March 22th

I went to see her again today. When I open the sheet, I wasn't prepared for the sight of her decomposed body. Time had fucked me again. She had turned into a fatty pool of slime. When I went to move her around to see if I could yet discern her lips still, she broke. Her shoulder bone protruded through where her skin had dissolved. I cried. I can't bear to watch her suffer any more. Come daylight I will bury her.

March 29th

Today I had a thrill so wonderful. The past week nothing seemed to give me the pleasure that I needed to cum. The Asian whore willingly offered me asshole. I'm able to pound into her for hours on end without loss of my erection. I've allowed her to sleep in the bed with me for warmth. I woke up last night in a cold sweat. Her breathes had become extremely loud. I could her heart beat like drums in my ears. It infuriated me that she made those horrible sounds and wouldn't stop. When I straddled her and begin to slap her face, she began to scream. Her screams overwhelmed the sound of her heartbeat. I let her go to wash her face. She put on more lipstick, I can't stand to see her plain pie face. Her lips were so vibrant. A picture of my last love wrapped in the sheet came to me as the Asian whore put on her lipstick. I sat on the side on the bed, while she used her mouth on me afterwards. I watched and enjoyed as she gagged, then I held her head in place and came.

April 5th

The Blond one came to me on her own today. I was on my way to the barn. She begged me to take her with me. I didn't. The things in the barn are for me. They are mine. Those are my things.

April 12th

The police were here. They claimed to have received a complaint about a foul smell from my property. I asked who complained but they didn't say. They wanted to walk around the property. I refused. I told them that deep freezer had broken while I was on vacation. A substantial amount of meat had gone to waste. I told them that it had already been removed. Again, I asked who had complained. So that I might at least send them a basket and apology. The officer noted that there was no smell in the air then told me to send the basket to the house on the right.

April 19th

I went to Detroit this weekend. Such beautiful women walked the streets half naked. I rented a car and drove along the Red Light District of Cass Corridor to find some company. The selection has changed drastically. A few of them were clearly too high to even show the kind of fear I desired. I went back to the hotel alone. The desire has become a hunger. I must.....

Chapter Nine

April 26th

They need me to come back. I'll leave tonight.

May 3rd She was beautiful. I'm obsessed. She will love me or teach me love. I followed her and saw what she did to that woman. How I wished she would do that to me. My dick grew so hard that I left her a gift in the rose bush. I never do that to myself. On the plane when I thought of her, my loins began to burn with desire The stewardess came along with drinks and peanuts. She saw my dick bulge as I tried to hide it with the small airline pillow. She offered to meet me a half hour in a hotel room when the plane landed in Dallas and I agreed. She gave me the information. The stupid cow never asked my name. I will watch the news from the resort for when they find her. I used a condom with her. She waited for me and when I got there she immediately closed the door behind me. I unzipped my pants and watched as she sucked me deep into her throat. I was about to release, when she stood up and pulled her skirt up. She presented her body to me from behind and leaned on a dresser. I'm glad she did it that way. I was able to watch as I pulled her sweater up around her neck. She looked back at me expectantly.

When I was done, I used a tissue from the dresser and put the condom inside. The thought to put her into the tub and wash her occurred to me. When I turned her over, blood ran from her orifices. Her eyes were swollen shut and her nose had disappeared into her skull, it left only a small flap of flesh that protruded. I left.

Chapter Ten

Synz was still on the floor when she heard a car door slam. Her heart raced. She took the diary and hid it under her side of the mattress. She sat on the spot where she'd put the book.

Just then Dan opened the bedroom door. Synz stretched her arms high in the air. He looked at her and smirked. She returned a weak half-hearted smile.

Dan walked into the bathroom and turned on the shower. Synz had begun to notice that he bathed constantly. He'd take as many as five showers a day. When he returned to the bedroom, Synz had already gotten up to pass him clean underclothes. Dan took them from her and softly patted the back of her hand in return.

He pushed the door partially closed behind him. She thought about the recorder. She couldn't recall if she had put it back. Synz walked over to window on his side of the room. She checked to see if he could see her. Synz could see the edge of the recorder box as it stuck from under the ledge of the stand. Dan called out to her to join him.

Synz sauntered over to the stand and kicked the device farther under the nightstand from view. She went to the bathroom door and shoved it open. Dan gripped the edge of the shower curtain and looked out. Water dripped from his hair into his face. Synz laughed as he squinted.

"Open the curtain Dan." Synz said.

"Are you going to get in with me?" Dan asked.

"I told you to open that damn curtain right now. Why are you asking me questions? Just do what I said."

Synz watched as Dan slowly pulled the curtain open. His erection stood stiff and ready. Dan's chest expanded while the water pelted his skin. She lowered her gaze to his crotch. The thought that he may have stuck it in a corpse sickened her.

"You know what I want to see don't you." Synz asked.

"I don't want to do that. Get in the shower Sinclair. I want you." Dan said.

"Grab it. Stroke it and make me want you."

"If you would just…."

"I said grab it or I'm leaving this room."

"Like this."

Dan circled his large hands around his shaft and tugged at it half-heartedly. He looked at Synz. She sat on the toilet and crossed her arms. Synz licked her thick full lips. Dan gawked as her the tip of her tongue showed him just a sliver of pinkness. Dan hand began to move faster.

Synz stood up and pulled her breasts from her gown. She let the soft melons waggle as she jerked on the hardened nips. When she bent her head down and took her nipple into her own mouth, Dan groaned. While he watched her suck her nipple, Dan fought the urge to spill spew cream all over the shower wall.

"I want you." Dan moaned.

"People in hell want ice water. Finish your shower and meet me in the living room." Synz replied.

"What about my needs?"

"Stop whining and do what I asked."

Synz pulled her gown back over her breasts and stood up. She paused for a minute while Dan tugged furiously at his pole. Synz reached in the shower and slapped his hand. Dan flinched.

"What did I do?" Dan whined.

"Stop it, I don't want you cum. Just wash yourself and get out of the shower. I've a surprise for you.'" Synz said.

Synz went out of the bathroom, through the bedroom and then made her way down the stairs to the living room. She sat on the sofa and massaged her temples. Her mind had begun to race through what she'd read from Dan's diary. She immediately tried to figure out the implications. Until Synz could finish and read all that was in there, she had no idea exactly what it meant. Nevertheless, she'd already decided that Dan wouldn't touch her again.

An idea had finally formed in her mind. Synz stretched across the couch and grabbed the phone. Quickly, she dialed the numbers of an old associate. The phone rang several times before Monique answered.

"Hello." Monique said.

"Hey, how are you?" Synz asked.

"Good and you? I haven't heard from you in a while, what's up with you?"

"I'm as good as can be expected. I recently got married, no kids yet, and I'd love to get a chance to take you to lunch and catch up sometime. That's not why I called though. Is Candy available?"

Chapter Eleven

"I sent her out on a run over at the Glass House on Eight mile. She should be finished though, why?" Monique asked.

"I wanted to her to swing by here, if she's not booked already. I'll make sure she makes a nice tip if she can be here in the next half hour." Synz said.

"Send her to you? I didn't know you got down like that?"

"It's not for me. Look, as long as I've known you, I've never asked questions about what you do. It's a gig for your girl, so let's keep business in its place alright? Can she make it or not?"

"I'll send her right over."

"Good, here's the address."

Synz recited the address to her. The women made plans to meet up when their schedules would allow it. Synz hung up the phone. There was little for her to do but wait.

She leaned back on the sofa and relaxed as much as she could. She closed her eyes and breathed in deeply. Synz heard footsteps descend the stairs. She opened her eyes just in time to see Dan stroll into the living room.

He hadn't bothered to dry off completely, but instead had wrapped himself in a thick fluffy towel. Dan walked over and sat on the couch next to Synz feet. Water rolled from his chest down to the edge of the towel and he wiped it away with his hand.

"I'm done. Where do you want me?" Dan asked.

"Stay right there. Your surprise should be here any minute now." Synz said.

It had been almost forty minutes, before Synz heard a vehicle pull up in the driveway. She jumped up and raced to the door. Dan heard Synz breathe a sigh. He looked on curiously as Synz fumbled with the locks to open the door.

He sat up and gripped the towel tightly. When Synz finally managed to swing the door open, he watched as another woman stepped across the threshold into the house. She reached out to hug Synz. Dan watched as his wife backed up. Instead, she swung her arm toward the couch where Dan was.

The woman walked over to Dan and spoke softly. He nodded at her and leaned to see Synz where was. Synz was headed to him. Synz reached around the woman and pulled her jacket off and let it fall to floor. Dan stared on as Synz began to undress the woman.

"Dan this is Candy, Candy this is Dan." Synz said.

By the time Synz came around the woman and tugged at her shirt, the woman raised had her arms. When Synz went behind her and unsnapped her bra, Candy's massive breasts spilled out and hung like long, over-filled, balloons. Synz reached around the woman and lifted her heavy melons and jiggled them.

"Surprise Dan." Synz said.

Chapter Twelve

Dan continued to sit. Synz leaned over and whispered in the woman's ear. Candy nodded enthusiastically. Synz stepped aside the woman, while the woman kneeled in front of Dan.

Synz sat on the couch next to Dan. She watched as Candy lifted the towel that covered his loins. Synz grasped Dan's face and turned his head until his eyes met hers. She peered into his pupils until he closed his eyes.

"Look at me Daniel." Synz said.

Dan's eyelids flew open at the sharpness of her voice. He tried to contain his groans, as he felt Candy suck him deep into her mouth. Every part of him wanted to close his eyes and just enjoy the incredible blowjob the woman had begun. Synz hand on his face wouldn't allow it.

He shaft filled almost immediately as Candy slurped on his dick. He felt her fingers gingerly grip his sac and tug firmly. As Candy's mouth moved halfway down the length of him and stopped, Dan humped to go deeper. When he moved his hand to shove her head down on him, Synz smacked his fingers roughly.

"Stop it." Synz said.

"It feels so good, if she would just swallow it a little more, I can cum." Dan said.

"What did I tell you? You are going to sit here and take what the fuck I allow you to have. No more and no less. Until you learn to accept what I say, shit is going to be very bad for you. Do you understand me? Sit still and let her do this."

"Okay."

Synz ran her hand through Candy's weave and pushed her head down further onto Dan's member. She watched as the woman's jaws collapsed into a tight, wet vacuum. Dan closed his eyes for a brief second and Synz tightened her grip on his face in response. Candy gagged on Dan's dick and struggled to back up from the thickness as it invaded the depths of her throat.

When Synz at last let go of Candy's head, the woman increased her speed and bobbed her head furiously in Dan's lap. Synz watched Dan's eyes as water pooled in the corner. A few minutes later, Dan bit his bottom lip and mewed.

Synz had dug her nails into his face. Dan's body stiffened and Candy re-doubled her efforts on his dick. She sucked hard on his pole. A glassy eyed Dan grimaced, as he felt the juices pulled from the bottom on his balls. Synz smirked, while she observed Dan literally be robbed of his male nectar.

Candy swallowed loudly. Synz continued to hold on to his cheeks while his body jerked with spasms of delight. At last, he relaxed and slumped down on the sofa. Candy let his shaft fall from her lips before she wiped her mouth with the back of her hand. Then the woman sat on her haunches and awaited further instructions.

"Dan, tell her thank you. She needs fifteen for the short notice." Synz said.

"I'm not thanking a whore for sucking me off. I'll give her ten dollars and she can get the hell out of my house." Dan replied.

"Then you'll owe that whore one thousand four hundred and ninety dollars. Pay the woman you cheap bastard."

Dan sat up and looked at Synz. His brow wrinkled and he scowled. She folded her arms defiantly and stared back at him. Dan shook his in the negative firmly.

"You can wag that noggin of yours until it falls off, but you're gonna pay the woman one way or the other." Synz said.

"Have you lost your mind? I thought you meant fifteen dollars, not fifteen hundred. There is no such thing as a fifteen thousand dollar blow job. I could have picked up a crack head and gotten a blowjob for eight bucks." Dan yelled.

"You could have done before you married me. Now, if you do that then clearly I would have to see that as infidelity on your part. That might hurt my feelings. This I sanctioned and clearly I think you deserve the best blowjob possible. There's no reason for you to be picking up common street walkers. Pay her."

"If I do, I'm gonna give her a check."

"Go ahead, then she'll have your real name, bank account and routing numbers, address, and proof that you paid a hooker. That ought to be good for a scandal and lawsuit later."

"Aww man, this is some bullshit. I didn't call her in the first place. What was the point of marrying you if I have to pay for it?"

"I wasn't looking for a hubby, you wanted a wife."

"I don't like this shit. I don't like this one bit."

"Sorry to hear that, however the woman still needs her little money. Unless there's something else you want from her that is. Otherwise she's got things to do and time is money."

"Why you arrogant little…."

"Dan, don't say it. I might have been a small business woman; nevertheless I still believe business is business."

"But I didn't ask you for this. This was supposed to be a surprise for me."

"Surprise"

Dan huffed as he snatched up the towel and covered him. He almost knocked Candy over as he leaped up to go and get the money. Synz tried to subdue her smile as he stomped up the stairs. Dan mumbled and cursed under his breath along the way.

Chapter Thirteen

"I can finish what all he gets for fifteen hundred, if you want me to. I usually only charge two hundred for some head. Do you get down with women? I could get you off too." Candy said.

"Would you shut the fuck up? Hell no, you're not putting your mouth on me." Synz asked.

"I didn't want to get in trouble later for over-charging."

"I tell you what. Invest that two first hundred and buy yourself something nice with rest."

"Invest? In what?"

"I don't know, shit condoms or something you use every day, like soap or something."

"I'll think about it."

Dan came down the stairs and walked over to Candy. He shoved a wad of crumpled bills in her hand. Synz winked at Candy as she stood up and headed to the door. Dan quickly walked over to the door and opened the door. He was anxious for his expensive surprise to leave.

She'd barely made it across the threshold of the door before Dan had slammed it. He turned to Synz and looked her up and down. She'd managed to get under his skin in way no one had done before now. At the moment he was torn between the urge to strangle her and the need to see what else she had in store for him. The latter need won out yet again.

Chapter Fourteen

"You know Synz; I had hoped that you'd be more open to me. Maybe even a little more honest. That was pretty shady on your part." Dan said.

"I don't know what you mean by shady Dan. How much more open can a wife be than to put her own needs to the sides for her man? Actually, I found that quite sexy and I can't believe you're so selfish. It's like you're unwilling to do anything that might make me happy. Before now you've jumped at the chance to have a strange woman suck you off. Now it's wrong. Make up my mind already." Synz said.

Dan opened his mouth to rebut what Synz had said. She stood up while his mouth opened and closed several times. Synz sashayed away and headed to the kitchen to find something to drink. Dan stood there and gritted his teeth.

After a few minutes, he went into the kitchen. He saw Synz bent over as she rummaged through the bottom of the refrigerator. Dan walked up and gripped a handful of her plump behind. When Dan came to he was laid out on the floor with carrots around him.

He reached up and grabbed his head as he sat up. His temple throbbed and he winced. He looked around and saw Synz at the stove. Slowly Dan made his way to his knees and then to his feet.

"You okay love?" Synz said.

"What the hell?" Dan asked.

"Sorry about that. You startled me while I had that bag of carrots in my hand. I tried to wake you up though. Do you want mushroom in your omelet?"

"I think you did that on purpose."

"I think you scared me on purpose. That was a natural reaction on my part. I already apologized, now would like one toast or two?"

Dan was furious. Determined to teach Synz a lesson, Dan decided he needed to smack her up and get her in line. Angrily he marched towards the stove. He reached out to grab her by the hair.

When Dan woke up his the back of his head pounded in pain. The cold tile caused him to shiver. His naked ass had nearly frozen and his sac rested uncomfortably on a full length carrot. Dan rubbed the back of his and tried to focus. The room seemed dim to him. He finally realized that Synz had left the room and turned off the light.

Dan felt a pain in his foot as well. He pulled the tender limb up into his lap for a closer inspection. His big toe nail was hung off to the side and dangled. He noticed and orange discoloration on the sole of his foot. Dan had slipped on a stray vegetable in his attempt to put Synz in her place.

Dan sighed. It took him while to get himself upright and stand. He limped up the stairs headed to the bathroom, in search of a first-aid kit and some aspirin. When Dan entered the bedroom, Synz was in the mirror, fully dressed.

He fumed as she put a layer of gloss across her lips. Her hair was pinned up in a twist. She'd put on a very snug flower print sheath dress with clear open-toed sandals. Dan gulped as he stood in the doorway naked and wounded. At that moment, she was the epitome of all that he thought his wife should be.

"How was your nap?" Synz quipped.

"I don't want to talk to you right now." Dan said.

"What are you mad at me for? You saw those carrots on the floor. All you had to was to pick them up. Did you eat breakfast?

"Oh I can't believe this day? So far, I been sucked off by an overpriced whore, knocked out cold by a bag of veggies, and bashed unconscious on a floor I paid for. I'm gonna shower and go back to bed."

"You don't want breakfast?"

"Synz, leave me alone right now."

"Okay, I'm going downstairs and take out something for dinner or should I make reservations?"

"I don't care what you do. I'm starting to believe you are bad luck,"

"Me? Really? That's insulting. I've done nothing this morning but try to please you. Who's being ungrateful now?"

Synz touched up her eye shadow while Dan limped into the bathroom. It wasn't long before she heard him turn on the water. She put off her next move, until she was sure he'd had time to get into the tub. Synz quickly dropped to the floor and crawled on Dan's side of the bed.

She ran her hand under the edge of his nightstand. Synz was search of the recorder. Her fingers had barely touched the tip of the device when she heard Dan call out to her. She dropped her head onto the floor and sighed before she stood up.

Chapter Fifteen

"What Dan?" Synz yelled.

"I hurt my toe really bad. Do you think I should wrap this up or go see a doctor?" He asked.

"You're an adult. What do you think?"

"What's the point of having a wife, if you're not going to help me with anything?"

"Hey buddy; you're the one made the decision that I'd be a good wife. I objected as much as possible. Since, you asked though, I'd go to the doctor. You know to avoid an infection or something."

"Will you drive me? My foot is swelling up."

"You really want me to drive you. How about I just call a ride for you?"

"Would you?"

"I'm on it."

Synz picked the phone and dialed four one-ones. She waited until the operator came on.

"Checker cab please." Synz said.

After the operator had connected her to the cab company, Synz requested a taxi to the house. She informed Dan that a cab would be there shortly. Dan rushed out, still wet and slipped into the clothes he'd worn the day before. He hurriedly went to grab shoes when he'd realized that his foot had swollen to the point that he was unable to put his shoes on.

He sat on the side of the bed in frustration. Synz went over to him and saw that in fact his great toe had begun to take on a purplish hue. She clucked her tongue and went over to the dresser. Synz took out one of Dan's white tee-shirts. She rummaged through a basket on the dresser until she found a safety pin.

When she returned to Dan, she'd folded the shirt into a make-shift soft cast. Synz bent down and tenderly lifted his foot. She gently wrapped the fabric around his limb and pinned it into place. By the time Synz was done, they both heard a horn outside.

Synz braced herself and reached for Dan to help him to his feet. He rocked several times to avoid added pressure to his injured foot and stood on one leg and his heel. She held onto him while he steadied himself. Dan hobbled out of the door and hopped down the stairs on his own. Synz trailed behind him, to be sure that he'd made it into the cab.

Once Dan was in the cab, Synz waved him off. The childish lost look on his face tugged at her sensitive side. Synz almost went with him. Instead she opted to let him go it alone.

The thought once again occurred to her to pack what she needed and leave. In her gut, she known after what she'd read from his own mind, that Dan would stop at nothing to find her. She could see her family if she chose to, her mother knew that she was still alive and father knew where she was. For the first time in her life, she hadn't hid from them because she her wayward lifestyle. She didn't want him to believe she'd had much attachment to them, and that meant he had little reason to use them against her. This way for what ever legnth of time, she had the upper hand.

Chapter Sixteen

The moment the cab pulled away from the curb, Synz went back inside the house and locked the door. Synz all but fell, on the way up the stairs in a hurry to get to the bedroom. As soon as she arrived in the room, she went straight for her side of the bed. Synz reached under the mattress and pulled out Dan's diary.

She flipped through the first few pages to pick up where she'd left off. She'd sensed that Dan was peeved this morning. There wouldn't be another sexual romp in the hay with him after what she'd read the day before. The thought of his touch sickened her, as she held his handwritten confession.

It had become clear to her that he was mentally sicker than even she'd imagination. She recognized the blatant signs of necrophilia. Of all the fetishes she'd ever encountered, she was aware that this one wasn't simply incurable; it was one of the final fetishes. Synz could foresee the need to either turn Dan in or worse.

Ted Bundy had suffered from necrophilia as well. It was the thing that had made him over the top in terms of serial killers. Necrophiliacs enjoyed sex with dead bodies. There is no middle ground. They are turned on by the absolute power and control over their victims past life.

Synz thought of it in terms of a final fetish because, unlike other off-colored desires, this one resulted in death. The understanding that he was more complex, that she'd originally believed, chilled her to the core. Had he'd been a cross-dresser; she could have helped him pick clothes. Had he been pleasured by humiliation, bondage, discipline, or pain there were ways to placate those desires in private. Short of the purchase of a morgue to provide him with endless corpses, there was anything to be done with him.

Her head had begun to hurt before she'd started to read. To some degree what she'd read the day before seemed familiar and recent. Synz struggled to catch that clue that peeked in her mind and then disappeared before she could put it into place. She was aware that she held proof of something, but what?

She'd thought about how she'd met him. How she'd come to be his wife. Even his curious reaction when she'd let the other women go. Synz had certainly expected him to go ballistic when she'd done so, instead he seemed accept it.

She wondered to her if in fact the answer was inside the pages of this diary. She flipped the book to the last page. His last entry had been in December. Nevertheless, her heart told her that this wasn't where his dictation had started. There must be other diaries. The thought to pick up the phone and call the police immediately screamed in her head. Even at that, Synz comprehended that there was quite a few problems with that solution.

First, Dan could always claim that he wrote those things as a fantasy, that they were notes for a book, or they were thoughts that he'd had from a dream. Secondly, there was no mention of where he'd buried anyone. With no body or proof of a murder, his fantasies alone were no crime. Third, she'd married him. Dan could easily claim that the two of them had an argument and that Synz had made the story up in order to one up him.

Synz suddenly grasped what her true mission was. When she'd decided to let the women go, she'd done her duty as a mistress. The belief that everything happened for a reason was one that she'd accepted as a part of life. Synz forced herself to acknowledge that the hands of fate had chosen her to be there. Up to that moment, she'd assumed that it had been to free the broken hearted women he'd kidnapped and enslaved.

She'd only planned to stay married to him long enough to make sure that she done the math on what to ask for in a divorce. Just then the grandfather clock in hallway chimed one. The sound bounced around in her brain. The number seemed like it screamed inside of her. Synz knew that she'd missed an important piece of the puzzle.

A quiver in her gut told her to put the book away for now. It took her a full ten minutes to decide that she might want to hide it away from him, but not in her possessions. There was a chance that he might look for it. Should he find it in her possessions, he'd kill her and enjoy what she wouldn't let him have while she breathed. Disastrously, she now knew that would be perfectly fine with him. She was definite that she needed to hide the diary.

Synz remembered how her sisters had helped her. She quickly went into the bathroom. Synz searched for the access panel for the pipes and located it. She hunted the bathroom drawers for something to secure the diary inside the panel.

Even as she scoured the bathroom, Synz couldn't find anything that was suitable. She shuffled his razors and other items that he'd kept inside of zip lock bags around in the top drawer. Her frustration grew as Dan could return at any moment. She was about to give up when spotted a case that held readers glasses and idea formed.

Synz had seen Dan use the glasses to magnify hairs after he shaved. He'd attached a clip that he used to hang the glasses around his neck. After he plucked stubborn hairs and whatnot, Dan then took off the spectacles to apply astringent before he moved on to the next area. She'd finally found a reason to celebrate his diva-like tendencies, as she took the clip from his spectacles.

She dumped a zip lock bag that contained several pairs of tweezers and placed the diary inside of it. Synz clipped the first end on the bag and held it mid-air. After she was sure that the clip would support the weight of the book, Synz opened the panel. It took her less than a minute to wind the excess string around the drain pipe. She allowed the bagged book to hang down between the floor and the ceiling, and then carefully replaced the panel.

Chapter Seventeen

It was late in the afternoon when Dan returned. The sun had gone down and Synz had decided to prepare dinner for them herself. She had already ground up two Nye-time sleep aid tablets and put them in his mashed potatoes. Synz used fresh roasted garlic to flavor the concoction. Synz was determined that he would ingest it, even if she had to hand feed it to him.

When he came in, his head was wrapped and his foot was in a soft shoe. He informed her that he'd suffered a concussion as well as broken his toe. Synz held her composure as she helped him up the stairs. Dan hobbled to the bed and threw back the covers. Synz lifted his leg, so that he could slide further onto the mattress.

"I have to take pain pills every six to eight hours. They gave me prescription for them but I came straight here." Dan said.

"Let me get you some food in your stomach first, and then I'll figure out how to get those for you. I'd prefer that you had something in your system first before you start any heavy medication." Synz replied.

"You really do care about me huh? I thought you stayed because out of fear or to get your hand on my money or something? I've racked my brain to figure out why you haven't bolted yet."

"Maybe I appreciate all of what you've gone through to get with me. It's not every day a girl gets kidnapped, violated and married by an intensely, sexy, stud now is it?"

"You really appreciate my efforts?"

"Isn't that you wanted from Dan, my gratitude?"

"Well yes"

"Then why are you surprised? Don't answer that let me go your dinner."

Synz left Dan to get his tray. When she returned she sat on the side of the bed and began to feed him. Dan raised his arms behind his head and rested on them while his wife attended to him. She had virtually fed him every morsel of food on the plate, when Dan rose up.

"What's wrong Dan?" Synz asked.

"Nothing, I just remembered that I'd forgotten to put my necklace back on this morning. It fell behind the stand last night. I'll be sure to get it first thing in the morning. They gave me a lot of pain meds at the hospital and I'm tired and nauseas." Dan said.

Synz hand began to quiver slightly. She made her move to get up and take the empty tray to the kitchen. When Synz reached the middle of the stairs, she heard him retch loudly. She sped up her steps to be as far away as possible while he continued to vomit.

Synz felt as though she had given Dan enough time to finish his business, before she returned to the bedroom. She made her way to the bedroom door. When she stepped inside she gasped. The nightstand had been pulled from the wall and the bed was empty.

Chapter Eighteen

Her legs felt as if they were made of rubber. Synz had assumed that Dan had gone into the bathroom to clean up. She had to know. At a snail's pace Synz ventured further into the room.

She'd barely managed to clear the bedroom door, when it slammed shut. Synz could feel that he was directly behind her. Instinctively, she took two giant steps forward before she turned to face him. Dan stood behind the door with a wild eyed glare. He blinked several times as if he couldn't focus his vision.

Foam bubbled from the corners of his mouth and he teetered to balance himself. Dan jiggled his head. He lunged at Synz. When she moved he landed face first on the foot of the bed.

"Synz help me please. I can't see. I can't go to bed like this. I taste vomit. Oh my god, I taste hell in my mouth." Dan pleaded.

Synz sighed. He wasn't out to get her as she feared. He seemed to have a bad reaction to the mix of sleeping pills and pain medications. Dan had run into the furniture as he attempted to find the bathroom. No doubt he'd thought the bedroom door was the bathroom door.

He babbled a few more minutes then began to snore. Synz fought the urge to run from the house. She was sure that Dan was one of the world's most prolific and diabolical serial killers. Even as he slept, it brought her no comfort.

It was only a matter of time before his temporary wounds healed. It came down to a number of days rather than months, until he was whole again. Ahead of Synz lay the choice of a lifetime. Should she decide to free herself, she understood she could unleash a narcissistic, necrophiliac back into the world unchecked and unhinged. It she stayed, there was a chance that before she could make sure that something was done about him, his urge would return with a vengeance. Ought the latter to be true, Synz was there next to him, an easy target.

She grasped his arm and attempted to pull him farther on the bed.

Chapter Nineteen

It was eleven a.m. when Dan at last began to stir. His foot throbbed from the pooled up blood. Synz had found that she was unable to move him and spent an hour on the side of the bed and watched him sleep. The position of his body after he'd fallen had caused his legs to hang off of the mattress.

Synz under eyes were puffy from exhaustion. Once she was sure that Dan was soundly into slumber land, she'd gone into the bathroom and locked it. Synz retrieved the diary and read more of the pages before she could no longer stand the gruesome details. What she'd read had made her fear sleep.

May 10th

How absolutely hypocritical of the media and the family of that wanton tramp! It took three days for anyone to notice that she was amiss, let alone dead. I watched to be sure that I'd made no mistakes. The police look confused and befuddled. It's so delightful me to see them stand there with cameras shoved in their faces, while they admit that they don't know anything. Her husband is such a mousy creature. It's no wonder she opened her legs to any man that would have her. He was on National Television and cried like a menopausal bitch. I poured me a scotch, and scratched the nuts that I banged into her pliant ass, while he blubbered like a girl in front of the world. They finally said her name, which is my first I had learned of it. Shamokin Davis-Jones. The casket will be closed due to the damage to her face. I disagree strongly with that. They hail her as if she was some kind of earnest citizen and worthy member of the community. The woman met a total stranger and offered herself completely. I won't get caught because other than me on that flight, there is nothing to connect me to her. It was her room. How is she a victim? I was the one subjected to temptation of her slutty ways. She never asked my name, if I was married, had kids, sick parents, or was I diseased? That stupid cunt of a spouse of her's would have greeted her with sloppy wet tongue kisses on her safe return. Probably would have dropped to his knees to bring her to pleasure with his tongue.

Never even as much as slightly aware that I, a total stranger, had throat-fucked her as they kissed, or known that he'd sucked my dick by default when he put his mouth on her. I detest people like that. They swear on all that just and right that they have been wronged. I didn't make them prey. They have victimized me. It's not my fault that she didn't live pass her effort to use me for my sexual skill. No harm would have come to her, had she not been in the way.

The airline would give her a posthumous award for service, while they offer money for the capture of her killer. How deceitful. The realistic wives of the world should take up donations and send them to me. I've relieved them of one more slut that has no regard for the sanctity of marriage. Freed up one more asshole, that will need a wife and has a pocketful of insurance money.

May 17

Last night I slept fitfully. I continue to see her in my dreams. The short brown skinned woman. I awoke hard and ready to thrust my spear deep inside of her. I wonder if she has quiet soft orgasms or does she moan and flail about in the throes of her release. She seems as if she would whimper softly and clutches her man tightly for warmth and protection. I have to go Bangkok this afternoon. I hope the urge doesn't overwhelm me.

May 31st

I spent two weeks out of the country. I had occasion to visit the place where I'd met Yandi. The streets were alive in the marketplace. The kiosks deal temptations abound at every cart. The geisha girl on the corners that offer sucky-sucky is the worst myth ever. The women there are not all shy or overtly sexual. Many of them are highly intelligent and skilled in various areas. I didn't mingle with the native women. Although my hosts had made it plain that whatever I desired was easily within reach. They have finally seen the logic of my proposal. One of my American companies will now export goods to the Bangkok market.

June 6th

The thought of this woman is has drove me to edges of craziness. Last night, I spent hours awake, as I poured over reports that concerned the Real Estate Market in Michigan. After a few calls, I finally found and investigator to get the job done. It was almost two a.m. when the urge hit me. Instead, I called an Escort service. I find that there are times that I'm aroused when a woman is aggressive with me first. I wonder why? Mother never spanked me and father was never home to do so. When the whore arrived, I was on the couch in my robe. She wasn't an attractive woman but she was large and yellow. This will be the last time I call on that service. After I let her in, she stripped down to her underwear. Her breasts sagged so that I inquired her age. She claimed that she was twenty six. I chuckled at the absurdity of the lie. They grey wiry hairs that peeked from the rim of her panties said otherwise.

She wasted no time to reach inside my housecoat and touch me. In a few scant moments, I was hard and thrusted into her plump jaws. The head was sloppy at best. I decided it might be better to spread her ass and have that. She readily agreed and stood up to take off her panties. I saw that the seat was filled with slimy yellow gunk, as they fell to the floor. After she stepped from the nasty panties and bent over to show me her target, I gagged. An intense odor wafted from her crevices. When she reached behind her and spread her cheeks, the putrid smell rose from her like steam. It was a stench that made rotted flesh smell like freshly cooked food. Her loosely wrinkled anus was almost covered with hair. Due to fairness of her skin, I could clearly see skid marks where she had attempted to wipe away feces, probably in a drunken haze. My erection fell. I closed my robe tightly and paid her to leave. I let her out of the front door and peeked through the blinds to be sure that she'd left my property. I watched her go to a light blue mini-van and bang on the window. Two little heads appeared and the one of them struggled to open the latch.

If I hadn't lost my stiffness because of her body odor, those children may have had a chance at a normal life. Instead, they are forever trapped in her stench. A smell so atrocious, that it will hang about their heads for the rest of their lives.

June 13th

The report on the Detroit woman has arrived. My dick grew as I held onto the envelope. The investigator wanted to stay and go over the report with me. I paid him in cash and asked him to leave immediately. He'd managed to take several photos of her from her "ordinary" life. I was surprised to see that she buys her own groceries, takes trips to the post office, and cuts her own grass occasionally. Those are menial chores that she'd never be allowed to do with me. I searched to find the name of her lover or possibly her pimp. It seems by all appearances that she doesn't have a man in her life. How can she be single? I think that the agent has overlooked something.

I've found a property in the area that I saw her in. It is suitable for its purpose. I wired the check to close the deal. Next week I will go there and furnish it, to begin to lay the foundation for my plan. I can't afford to let this chance slip by me. Even her walk says that she can help me be whole and fulfilled. There is an ache in my belly now when I look at the photos of her. I took some Pepto and lay down. When I looked at the pictures again, the sensations returned. I don't understand this.

I received a communication from a woman I'd known in school. Dana Newsome contacted me and asked when I returned to Boulder, CO, if I would pay her a visit. She'd married a fellow, Mark Glitch right off from High school. He'd found her in the brothel. If memory serves me, she'd not only given him a case of sick nuts, but she'd spread the plague among most of his associates. The last time I'd seen her she worked in a hotel. Her days were spent on her knees as she scrubbed toilets and bathtubs behind the general population. I'd run across her at the bar after her shift one night in the lobby of the hotel. She'd told me she'd just been fired. A guest of the hotel had left behind an unopened bottle of Remy Martin. She'd drank it and become ill. Dana admitted that her supervisor had search for her and found her in a room, asleep on a toilet, with her drawers around her ankles filled with vomit. I've no desire to see her again. I'd fucked her a week after she'd pledged herself to Mark, for a dime bag of weed and cab fare.

Synz heard the phone ring. She quickly checked the bathroom latch and then replaced the book back into its secret location. After she was sure that the room appeared normal, she shut down the water and opened the bathroom door. The phone rang and Dan hadn't as much as moved his head towards the sound.

Synz walked over to the nightstand. The trill sound of the bell seemed to beg her to answer. As if guided by an unseen force, Synz lifted the receiver from the cradle. She cleared her throat and put the phone to her ear.

"Hello" Synz said.

"Dan?" Lori whispered.

"No. He's asleep. This is Sinclair. Would you like me to wake him?"

Chapter Twenty

"You are who I'd wanted to speak with. Listen to me. Don't have any children with my son. Please. Let his tainted blood go the grave. You are in a position to do what I never could, stop him. Ezra's father eventually murdered his mother. He'd come home and caught her in bed with another man. Dan's grandfather also killed his own father. I can't rest knowing that you married him. When love calls, I suppose that we women tend to fall for the fairytale. Nevertheless, Ezra father hated competing with his father. When he came home and caught him in bed with his wife, he murdered them both. The man went to a bar and ordered several drinks, then called the police and told them what he'd done. His only excuse was that he loved his wife Linda and he'd be damn if he'd allow their father to continue to sleep with his woman. Don't you see? Ezra murdered his sister and father because they were lovers too. Ezra went insane when he realized that Dan's father might not have been his son after all. Help me please. When I opened myself to Dan's father it took almost a decade to see that I had in fact opened Pandora's Box."

"I don't understand why you've told me this."

"Stop that bloodline. I was ignorant but you've yet to give birth."

"I've no intention of having children."

"It's too late for intentions."

"Huh?"

"Heed my warning. You can stop him. The way he acts around you is the only time I've ever seen of true emotions from him. As far as he can love, he's given it to you. My chest hurts so badly today. I must go and take my nitroglycerin for my heart. I've held on long enough to tell someone. It's no longer my burden. I...I..."

"Lori?"

Lori didn't answer. Shortly after Synz heard a thud then the phone disconnected. Synz woke Dan and told him to call his mother. Dan rolled his eyes and lay his head back down.

The nature of Lori's call had disturbed Synz. She'd begun to worry when Lori didn't call back. Synz pressed *69 and waited. A recorded message came on and stated that the line was busy and would be connected as soon as it became available. Synz sat on the mattress and hung on while she listened for the signal that Lori had been able to hang up the phone. It never came.

Chapter Twenty One

The sun had risen brightly in the afternoon sky when Synz heard the doorbell. Dan had since awakened, showered, and eaten a Philly Cheesesteak from Papa's Pizza. She was lounged on the sofa, when Dan came from the kitchen to open the front door. She was barely able to make out bits and pieces of the conversation Dan was in the middle of. He spoke in hushed tones, and then closed the door.

He walked over to the couch and sat next to Synz. She eyed his face, once again Synz searched for a clue to his emotional state. There was none. Dan leaned over and pulled her leg up into his lap.

"Who was that at the door?" Synz asked.

"The police" Dan replied.

"What did they want?"

"They came to tell me that Mother died this morning."

"Oh my goodness, what happened?"

"Stroke or something?

"Are you okay?"

"Yes"

One week later Synz stood next to Dan at his mother's graveside. Two women stood to the right of them and sobbed. It was apparent that the women were sisters. Their faces were close to identical. The minister had already delivered his final prayer and the crowd had begun to disperse.

The sun beamed hard down on the open hole. The Casket that held his mother's remains stood on a gurney next to the open grave. Dan held onto a single rose from her spray. Synz watched as the attendees placed a flower or card onto the box. The flower in Dan's hand seemed to glow in the sunlight. The weather was perfect for a picnic or afternoon sail. It belied the fact that death had come to this family.

Synz watched as one by one, people began to leave. Dan stayed firmly rooted in the same spot. The two women that had stood close by and wept openly had taken a break from their intense grief. Synz tugged on Dan's arm. He looked towards the gate at the people that left but he didn't budge.

With only five people left, Synz was ready to go. Just then one of the women that cried profusely before had walked around her and stopped nose to nose with Dan. Synz released his arm and put her hand on her hip. Dan didn't acknowledge the woman, even when the other woman came and grabbed her arm to drag her away.

"Daniel, may you rot in hell. You worthless son of a bitch, it's your fault that she's dead. Not as much as a tear on your face and she probably protected you with her last breath. That should be you in that casket. I will never forgive you for this. You took my mother from me." The woman screamed.

"Daniel, who was that woman?" Synz asked.

"Her name is Tracey. She's the eldest of my twin sisters." Dan said.

Synz was about him question him further when she clutched her belly. She'd gotten a sharp pain right under her navel. She felt sweat roll in between her breasts from the heat. She shifted uncomfortably as she tenderly tried wiped the water away. She winced as the material of her bra seemed to shrink. Synz thought it was time for her menstrual cycle and the twinge she felt were cramps.

In the confusion and stress of the day, she struggled to remember when her period had come last. She walked over to a tree in search of shade. Dan had sisters that he'd never mentioned was a bit of a shock to her. The pain in her lower abdomen had increased.

Chapter Twenty Two

Synz stood under the tree and muttered to her.

"Okay, I had my last one at the start of last month. Now wait, that was the end of the month before. Hold on, I know I just had just gone off two days before this shit started with Dan. The last cycle I've had was two months ago."

"Sinclair, I'm ready to go." Dan yelled.

Synz began to make her way to the car when she was accosted by a frail old woman on a cane. It seemed that the woman had suffered from some kind of debillating illness. Her left shoulder and side of her face had a droopy appearance. When she tried to speak her words were slurred and choppy. However, she had managed to grip Synz firmly with her left hand as she'd passed the woman on the way to the car.

"Lori..Lori said give this…to..to you. He did..it. He..took my baby…from us. I..hope..he rots..in..in hell." The woman stuttuered.

A spasm of coughs shook the old womans body. Synz was concerned that she exhausted her last few breaths with those few words. She reached out and took the envelope the woman had attempted to give her and held it up to open it.

"Not here, not in front of him." The woman admonished.

Synz nodded her head that she understood and then slipped the envelope into her handbag. She gently patted the old woman's hand and turned to make her way to the car. When she was in the car, she looked back over to the place where the woman had been to be sure she'd begun to make her journey to whatever ride awaited her. Synz fastened her seatbelt and gasped as the woman was nowhere to be seen. It her physical state, Synz doubted that she'd suddenly developed the ability to sprint off unnoticed. She could still clearly see the spot that she'd encountered her and no one lay in the grass, yet she was gone. Synz dcontinue to search through the car window for any sign of the woamn even as the car pulled into the dirt trail that led to cemetary gate. She reasoned she'd must have imagined the whole incident.

"What did that old bitch give you?" Dan asked.

"Huh, oh the old lady. It was a condolence card I think." Synz replied.

"When we arrive at the house, throw it away. I've no need for her sympathy."

"Sure, if you don't mind me asking, who is she?"

"Paula's mother."

"Of course Dan, I'll throw it away. I don't want you to communicate with another woman from your past. You are mine and mine alone."

Synz glanced out of the corner of her eye at Dan as she spoke. For a brief second, his face softened. He reached up and rubbed his forhead and then wiped the length of his face. Dan took his hand and brushed at his trousers absently. She glanced out of the window and then turned her head towards him just in time to catch a glimmer of a smile.

"If you say so, Synz. It what ever you want it to be. She'll never be a factor in our lives anyway. I can guarantee that. I'm yours to use as you will." Dan replied.

Stay connected to this author

www.inakat1.com

@inakat1 on Twitter

Inakat Publishing on Facebook